BIRD
RIES

Rush!
&
Tap, Tap, Tap!

DISCARDS

Early★Reader

First American edition published in 2021 by Lerner Publishing Group, Inc.

An original concept by Katie Dale
Copyright © 2022 Katie Dale

Illustrated by Angelika Scudamore

First published by Maverick Arts Publishing Limited

Maverick
arts publishing

Licensed Edition
Rush! & Tap, Tap, Tap!

Lerner Publications Company
An imprint of Lerner Publishing Group, Inc.
241 First Avenue North
Minneapolis, MN 55401 USA

For reading levels and more information, look up this title at www.lernerbooks.com.

Main body text set in Mikado. Typeface provided by HVD Fonts.

Library of Congress Cataloging-in-Publication Data

Names: Dale, Katie, author. | Scudamore, Angelika, illustrator. | Dale, Katie. Rush! | Dale, Katie. Tap, tap, tap!
Title: Rush! ; & Tap, tap, tap! / Katie Dale ; illustrated by Angelika Scudamore.
Other titles: Readers. Selections
Description: First American edition, licensed edition. | Minneapolis : Lerner Publications, 2021. | Series: Early bird stories. Early reader. Pink | "First published by Maverick Arts Publishing Limited"—Page facing title page. | Audience: Ages 4–8. | Audience: Grades K–1. | Summary: "A family rushes to reach their destination in one silly story and taps their way through their day—to the seeming annoyance of their neighbor—in another"— Provided by publisher.
Identifiers: LCCN 2020013612 (print) | LCCN 2020013613 (ebook) | ISBN 9781728417264 (lib. bdg.) | ISBN 9781728420448 (pbk.) | ISBN 9781728418049 (eb pdf)
Subjects: LCSH: Readers (Primary)
Classification: LCC PE1119.2 .D357 2021 (print) | LCC PE1119.2 (ebook) | DDC 428.6/2—dc23

LC record available at https://lccn.loc.gov/2020013612
LC ebook record available at https://lccn.loc.gov/2020013613

Manufactured in the United States of America
1-48984-49237-10/14/2020

EARLY BIRD STORIES

Rush!
&
Tap, Tap, Tap!

Katie Dale

Illustrated by
Angelika Scudamore

Lerner Publications ◆ Minneapolis

The Letter "R"

Trace the lowercase and uppercase letter with a finger. Sound out the letter.

Down,
up,
around

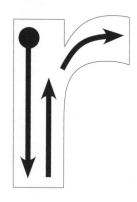

Down,
up,
around,
down

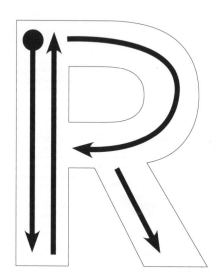

Some words to familiarize:

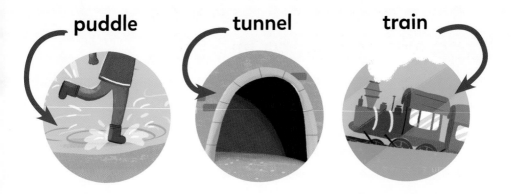

puddle   tunnel   train

High-frequency words:

go to off the

Tips for Reading *Rush!*

- *Practice the words listed above before reading the story.*
- *If the reader struggles with any of the other words, ask them to look for sounds they know in the word. Encourage them to sound out the words, and help them read the words if necessary.*
- *After reading the story, ask the reader what everyone got onto in the end.*

Fun Activity

Discuss other things that go "puff."

Rush!

Run to the hill.

Run to the puddle.

Puff! Puff! Puff!

Run to the tunnel.

Puff! Puff! Puff!

Run to the bus.

Puff! Puff! Puff!

Run to the train.

The Letter "T"

Trace the lowercase and uppercase letter with a finger. Sound out the letter.

Down,
lift,
cross

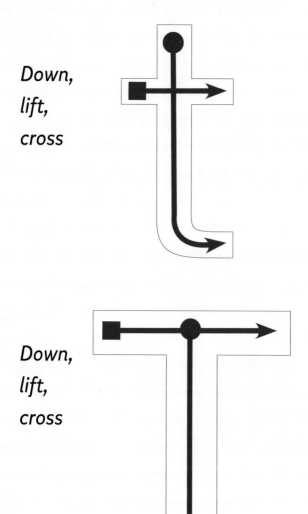

Down,
lift,
cross

Some words to familiarize:

Ben **Sam** **Sid**

High-frequency words:

can Mom Dad

Tips for Reading *Tap, Tap, Tap!*

- Practice the words listed above before reading the story.

- If the reader struggles with any of the other words, ask them to look for sounds they know in the word. Encourage them to sound out the words, and help them read the words if necessary.

- After reading the story, ask the reader why everyone was worried near the end.

Fun Activity

What noises can you make?

Tap, Tap, Tap!

Ben can tap.

Tap, tap, tap!

Nan can tap.

Tap,

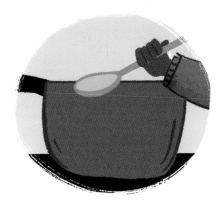

tap,

tap!

Sid can tap.

Leveled for Guided Reading

Early Bird Stories have been edited and leveled by leading educational consultants to correspond with guided reading levels. The levels are assigned by taking into account the content, language style, layout, and phonics used in each book.

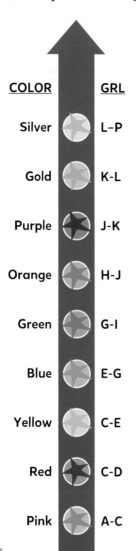

COLOR	GRL
Silver	L–P
Gold	K-L
Purple	J-K
Orange	H-J
Green	G-I
Blue	E-G
Yellow	C-E
Red	C-D
Pink	A-C